The Ninja Storm Story

Three misfit students are
the only survivors after evil
aliens attack their
Wind Ninja Academy.
Their Ninja master endows
them with the power of
the legendary
Super Megazords and
Power Rangers, and
Ninja Storm are born,
ready to save the world.

THIS POWER RANGERS NINJA STORM ANNUAL BELONGS TO

POWER RANGERS
NINJA STORM™

ANNUAL 2005

Contents

Prelude to a Storm 8

Power Rangers Profile
RED WIND RANGER 20

Power Rangers Profile
YELLOW WIND RANGER 22

Power Rangers Profile
BLUE WIND RANGER 24

There's No 'I' in Team 26

Boarding with Shane 38

Know Your Enemy ... 40

Thunder Strangers 42

Written by Brenda Apsley,
based on original scripts.
Designed by Jeannette O'Toole.

©&™BVS Entertainment, Inc. and
BVS International N.V.
All rights reserved.

Published in Great Britain 2004
by Egmont Books Limited,
239 Kensington High Street,
London W8 6SA

Printed in Italy
ISBN 1 4052 1389 2

abc
Kids™

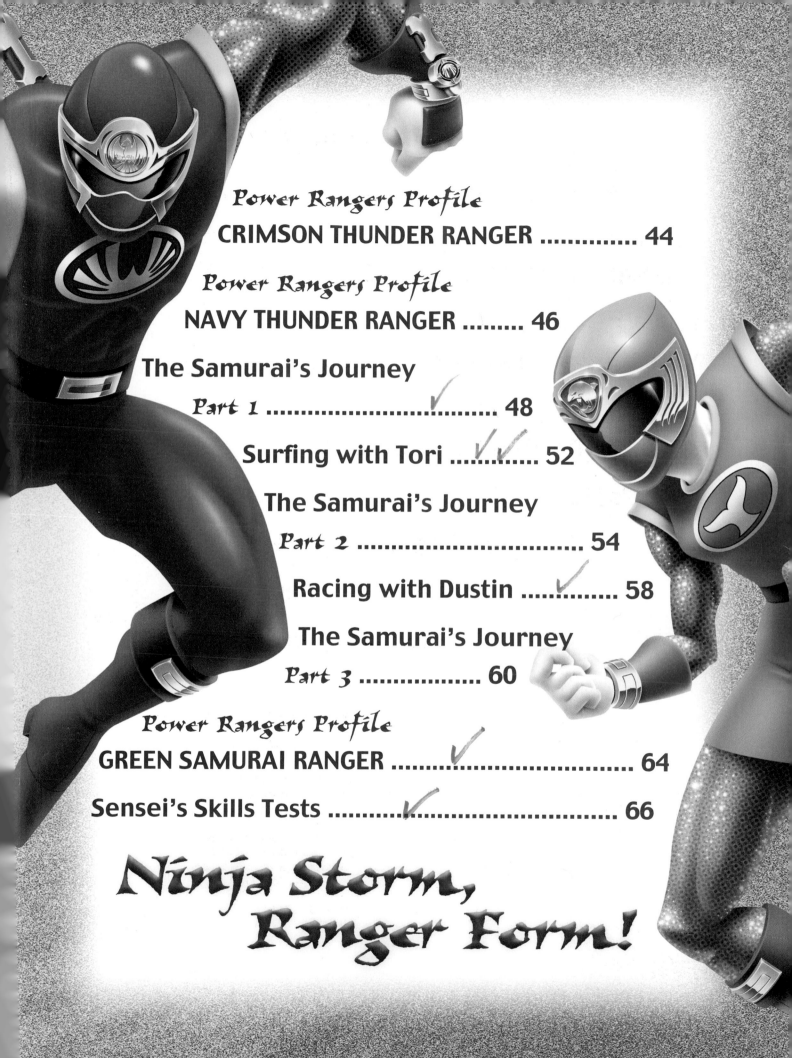

Power Rangers Profile
CRIMSON THUNDER RANGER 44

Power Rangers Profile
NAVY THUNDER RANGER 46

The Samurai's Journey
Part 1 48

Surfing with Tori 52

The Samurai's Journey
Part 2 54

Racing with Dustin 58

The Samurai's Journey
Part 3 60

Power Rangers Profile
GREEN SAMURAI RANGER 64

Sensei's Skills Tests 66

Ninja Storm, Ranger Form!

Prelude to a Storm

ROOAARR!!

JUMP!!!

SWOOOSSHH!!

It was time for Ninja class and as usual, Tori Hanson, Dustin (Waldo) Brooks and Shane Clarke were running late. All three were much too wrapped up in their extreme sports interests of surfing, skateboarding and motocross to keep an eye on the clock.

Tori was the first to realise what time it was and, after changing out of her surfing gear, she sat waiting for the others in her old van. "Where are they?" she said to herself. "Come on."

At last, Shane arrived on his skateboard. "You miss me?"

"Dream on," said Tori. "Where's Dustin? Last as usual."

He was. He climbed into the van through the back door, and hurled himself into the middle seat. "Move!"

"How come you guys are late every time?" said Tori. "I couldn't pull that off."

"That's because in any group – like, um, even the Power Rangers, I guess – there are different kinds of people," said Shane.

"Yeah," said Dustin. "There's like me, the mellow, reflective dude ..."

"... and I'm the risk taker," said Shane. "You, Tori, you're the reliable one."

"Are you comparing us to the Power Rangers?" said Tori. "You guys have to lay off the comic books. SERIOUSLY ..."

Tori parked the van in a clearing in the middle of a dense wood and the three friends walked into the trees.

"This place always creeps me out," said Dustin.

9

Shane glanced around as, out of nowhere, masked Ninjas dropped from the sky like over-sized raindrops. As they attacked, the teens' clothes morphed into Ninja uniforms, and they fought back. But their skills needed a little more work ...

Tori's attempt at running on water ended with her falling into the pond.

Dustin tried to burrow into the ground, but got stuck, and Shane's flight through the air ended in a heavy fall.

The teens were no match for the Ninjas, who had them cornered when a huge falcon landed nearby. It morphed into Sensei, their teacher.

"That's enough," said Sensei, and the attackers streaked off into the air. "I am very disappointed in you. We must discuss your lack of commitment to your Ninja training."

He led them through a portal behind a waterfall and into the other side of the dimension – Wind Ninja Academy.

"You fail to see the importance of punctuality," said Sensei. "I suggest you find a way to change that, or I will have no choice but to expel you. Now, go."

WOOOSSHH!!

SPLASSHH!!

UGHH!!

BZZ-ZZAM!!

HMMM!!!

"I don't know why you put up with them," said Cam, Sensei's son.

"I suppose that's why I'm the Sensei," said his father, then he paused and looked up to the sky. He sensed danger ... and it was coming his way.

•••

Next day, Tori and Shane were watching a skateboarding video in the Storm Changers extreme sports store and Dustin was in the workshop when all the clocks and watches went off. It was the Academy's alarm call, so they jumped into the van.

They were early for once, that is until Tori insisted they stop to help an old couple whose car had broken down ...

What they didn't know was that an alien space vessel had landed at the Academy, commanded by Lothor, and carrying his evil minions Zurgane, Marah, Kapri, Choobo ... and an army of Kelzak soldiers.

"Now is the time for revenge," Lothor told Sensei, firing a laser from his hand.

As they fought one on one, Zurgane and the Kelzaks attacked the Ninja students, who were no match for the evil warriors. Choobo unleashed energy spheres, which captured them one by one.

"Goodbye, Wind Ninja Academy!" said Choobo.

HYAH!!

AAAHH!!

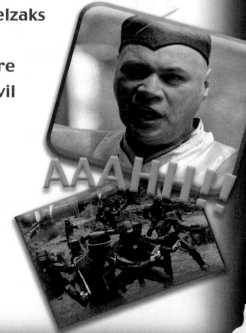

SWOOOSSHH!!

Tori, Dustin and Shane arrived just in time to see the Academy being sucked up into the sky, surrounded by a ball of energy. Then it just disappeared! They looked all around, but found only one person – Cam.

High above them, on the alien spaceship, Lothor was enjoying his victory. "Now that the last of the mighty Ninja Academies has been destroyed, planet Earth is ours."

But Zurgane had bad news for his boss. "There are still three Academy students unaccounted for."

Lothor glared at his general. "Clear the zone," he growled. "I want nothing left standing. NOTHING!"

Seconds later, laser beams streaked from the alien ship and explosions boomed and cracked around the teens.

KA-BOOM!!

"This way!" said Cam, leading them through a gap in the rubble into an underground area, the Ninja Ops room.

Tori looked around. "Amazing!"

"Dude!" said Dustin, gazing at a massive computer screen on the wall.

cCCREAKK!!

"This is like, some big secret?" asked Shane.

"Yes," said Cam.

"And there are times when secrets must be revealed," said another voice – Sensei's!

They turned towards their teacher's voice, but saw – a guinea pig, wearing his outfit!

"Dude!" said Dustin.

"He's stuck," said Cam.

"Stuck?" said Shane.

"Yes, stuck," said Sensei. "Observe."

Images appeared on the giant viewing screen. "This is Lothor," said Sensei. "Once a great Ninja, he was banished from Earth when his hunger for power lured him to the dark side. We fought just now, and when our energy fields collided, I was transformed into what you see before you."

Sensei continued his explanation as explosions filled the screen. "Now Lothor has returned again with an army that will take our planet, unless they are stopped."

"Who's gonna be dumb enough to try that?" asked Dustin.

Sensei paused. "An excellent question," he said, gesturing to his son. "The Morphers, Cam."

Cam hesitated. "Father, you're not serious?"

"We have no choice," said Sensei. Cam opened a box, revealing three glistening globes that crackled with energy. "Your Power Rangers Wind Morphers," he said.

"Yeah, right," said Tori.

ZZZZ!!!

Dustin took the Yellow Wind Morpher. "Child of the Earth, true to your heart, you will embody the powers of the Yellow Wind Ranger," said Sensei.

Tori took the Blue Morpher and Sensei said, "Fluid and graceful like the water, you will become the Blue Wind Ranger."

The Red Morpher was left for Shane. "Reaching for the stars, you will command the powers of the Red Wind Ranger," said Sensei.

He looked from one to the other. "From this time you will be known as the Wind Power Rangers, protectors of the Earth."

Dazed, and not a little confused, the teens looked at the morphers.

Tori tried to find the on–off switch.

"Does it have games?" asked Dustin.

Cam watched them. "Ladies and gentlemen, the defenders of our galaxy ..."

Suddenly, a Kelzak army with a hideous monster at its head appeared on the screen.

"Lothor's army is attacking," said Sensei. "You must intercept them. Call on your powers by saying the words 'Ninja Storm, Ranger Form'."

Still dazed, the teens nodded and went outside.

WOOOSSHH!!

After a couple of false starts, Dustin said, "Ninja Storm, Ranger Form! Power of Earth!" and Tori and Shane gaped as he morphed into Yellow Ranger.

"Ninja Storm, Ranger Form!" yelled Tori and Shane, and they morphed into Red Ranger and Blue Ranger.

"Power of air!" said Shane.

"Power of water!" cried Tori.

Their new powers were soon put to the test as the aliens attacked. The Rangers drew their Ninja sword weapons.

Red Ranger flew through the air, slashing at the Kelzaks and firing lasers from his morpher.

WWWHIRL!!

Blue Ranger blasted lasers at the Kelzaks as she ran across the water.

Kelzaks fell as Yellow Ranger burst amongst them from the ground in an explosion of mud and dust and fired at close range.

With the Kelzaks dealt with, the Power Rangers faced the monster.

HA-ZAP!!

"Wind!" said Red Ranger.
"Power!" said Blue Ranger.
"Rangers!" said Yellow Ranger.

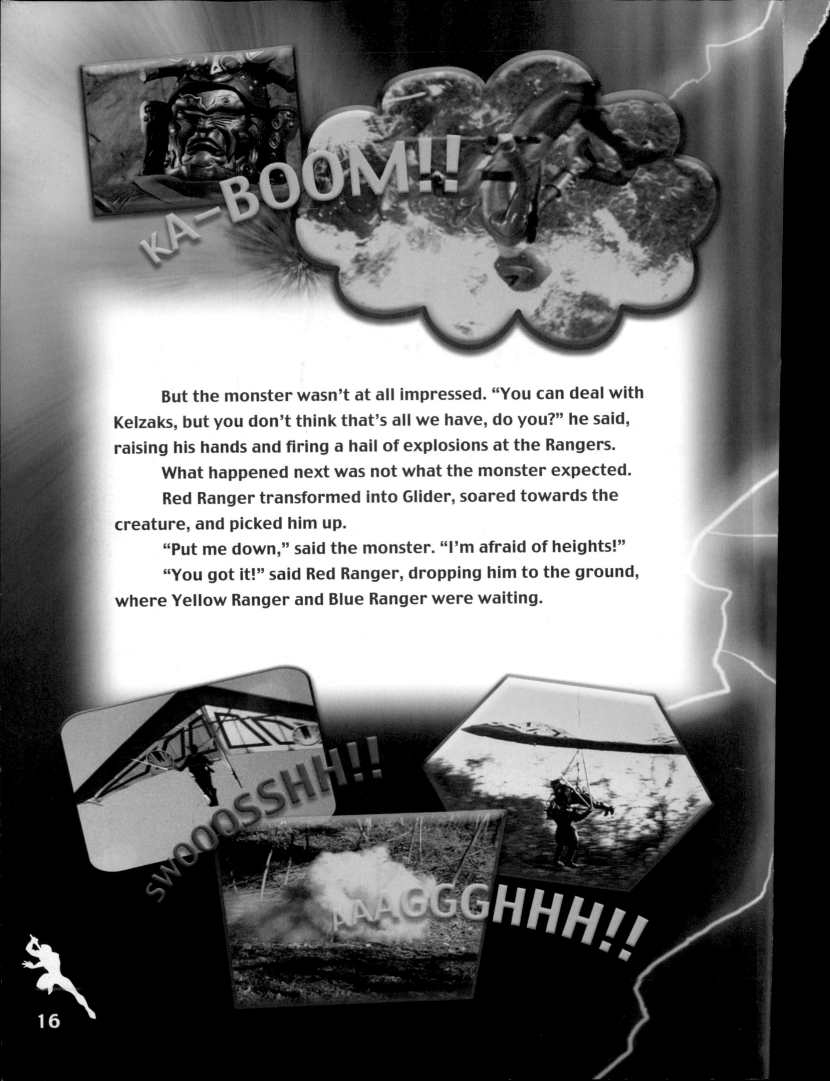

KA–BOOM!!

But the monster wasn't at all impressed. "You can deal with Kelzaks, but you don't think that's all we have, do you?" he said, raising his hands and firing a hail of explosions at the Rangers.

What happened next was not what the monster expected.

Red Ranger transformed into Glider, soared towards the creature, and picked him up.

"Put me down," said the monster. "I'm afraid of heights!"

"You got it!" said Red Ranger, dropping him to the ground, where Yellow Ranger and Blue Ranger were waiting.

SWOOOSSHH!!

AAGGGHHH!!

Red Ranger lifted the Hawk Blaster. "Hawk Blaster fired up!"

Blue Ranger lifted the Sonic Fin. "Sonic fin, sound off!"

Yellow Ranger lifted the Lion Hammer and said, "Lion Hammer, ready to roar!" as he smashed it to the ground with such force that the monster flew up into the air.

As he fell to the ground, Blue Ranger spoke to the Sonic Fin, and the monster spun in circles. Then Red Ranger aimed the Hawk Blaster, and a powerful beam hit the monster's body.

YEAH!!!

WWWHIR!!!

ZZZZ!!!

BAM!!!

The Rangers put their weapons together to form one: "Storm Striker!" Together they launched a ball of energy at the monster, scoring a direct hit – and the hideous creature exploded into a million pieces!

WOOOSSHH!!

BZZZ-ZZAM!!

BOOM! BOOM!!

When the smoke cleared, the Rangers looked at each other.

"That just happened, right?" said Red Ranger.

"I'm pretty sure it did," said Blue Ranger.

Yellow Ranger was impressed: "Awesome!"

● ● ●

Later, back in Ninja Ops, Sensei congratulated them, but he had words of warning, too. "There will be more battles in the future," he told them. "Lothor will not rest until the Earth is under his command, or until he is destroyed."

He looked from one to the other. "The future is in your hands, Power Rangers …"

POWER RANGERS PROFILE

FULL NAME:

Shane Clarke

RANGER DESIGNATION:

Red Wind Ranger

ZORD:	Hawk Zord
WEAPONS:	Ninja Sword, Laser Blaster, Hawk Blaster
GEAR:	Wind Morpher, Glider, Tsunami Cycle
SPORTS:	Skateboarding

CHARACTER:
As a Power Ranger, Shane is discovering his qualities as a natural leader. He realises that he and his friends need to work as a team if they're going to be successful in defending planet Earth.

SKILLS:
Shane loves doing daring airborne manoeuvres, either as a skateboarder or as a high-flying Ninja fighter. He fights with the power of the sky and the stars on his side, and pilots the awesome Hawk Zord.

Air!"

lammer

ycle

of comic
naive,
ople.

store, and
of
his power

FULL NAME:

Dustin (Waldo) Brooks

RANGER DESIGNATION:

Yellow Wind Ranger

ZORD:	Lion Zord
WEAPONS:	Ninja Sword, Laser Blaster, Lion [
GEAR:	Wind Morpher, Glider, Tsunami Cy
SPORTS:	Motocross

CHARACTER:

Waldo, or Dustin as everyone calls him, is a big fa[
books, and admits to being a thrill-seeker. He's a [
trusting sort of guy who tries to see the best in pe[

SKILLS:

Dustin works at Storm Chargers, an extreme sport[
races in motocross in his spare time. He is a master
underground-based fighting techniques, and gets [
from the Earth.

"Power of Earth!"

When an enemy strikes, Yellow Wind Ranger can call upon Lion Zord to help him.

Use the small picture of Lion Zord to help you colour the larger one.

POWER RANGERS PROFILE

FULL NAME:

Tori Hanson

RANGER DESIGNATION:

Blue Wind Ranger

ZORD: Dolphin Zord

WEAPONS: Ninja Sword, Laser Blaster, Sonic Fin

GEAR: Wind Morpher, Glider, Tsunami Cycle

SPORTS: Surfing

CHARACTER:
Tori is the logical, sensible member of the Power Rangers team. She's the one who organises Shane and Dustin, and is sometimes annoyed when they behave in what she thinks is a childish manner.

SKILLS:
Tori loves water, and spends her spare time out on the ocean, surfing. She mastered water–based fighting techniques during her training at the Wind Ninja Academy, and relies on the power of water.

"Power of Water!"

When an enemy strikes,
Blue Wind Ranger can call
upon Dolphin Zord to help her.

Use the small picture of
Dolphin Zord to help you
colour the larger one.

There's no 'I' in Team

The Rangers were in a strange desert dimension. Sensei had sent them to search for a magical 'Scroll of three', but they were not enjoying the job. Sensei wanted to test their ability to work as a team, so they were bound to each other at the wrist – and the cuffs they wore were painful.

When Shane moved forward he yanked the others with him. "It would be so much faster if we could split up," he said.

"And less painful," said Tori.

"What kind of scroll are we looking for, anyway?" asked Dustin.

Tori looked at the sea of pinky-red sand that surrounded them. "I think if we see a scroll here, that'll be it."

"OK ... there's one," said Dustin, pointing to a scroll that hovered in the air.

AAII!!

HYAH!!

KICK!!

"It's got a figure 3 on it," said Shane. "It says 'Stronger as one than three'."

They were about to reach for the scroll when an army of Kelzaks attacked. As they fought, one of the Kelzaks slashed at Shane, and cut him free from the others.

"Stay here," he told Tori and Dustin. "I'll get the scroll."

"No, wait!" said Dustin.

"Stop, Shane," said Tori. "We can't do this on our own."

But it was too late. When Shane turned around, his friends were surrounded. As he watched, they, the Kelzaks and the dimension dissolved away.

Back at Ninja Ops, Cam turned off the simulator that had created the training exercise.

"Well, that was ... below average," he said.

"Yes, Rangers, you are lucky this was just a simulation," said Sensei.

"We really need to practise this until you guys get it right," said Shane.

"WE get it right?" said Tori. "What about you?"

"If you think you can do better alone, go for it!" said Dustin.

Shane paused. "Maybe I will."

HUH?

Out in space, aboard Lothor's alien ship, Kapri and Marah were arguing. They couldn't agree on how to use their new PAM, the Personal Alien Manager used for calling up aliens from Lothor's army.

"You just erased!" said Kapri.

"So? I meant to!" said Marah, pressing a button.

As Mad Magnet appeared, the girls fought, and the PAM flew out of their hands. It hit Lothor on the head.

He was not pleased. "STOP!" he cried. "Magnet, show them what you can do."

Mad Magnet shot his ray at the girls, and they stuck together. Fast.

"I'll MAKE you two work together!" said Lothor.

KA-ZZZZ!!

HA-ZAP!!

Shane was on his skateboard when Kapri and Marah arrived on Earth.

The PAM screen flashed up the word RANGER.

"OK!" said Marah, pressing buttons. "Command ... send ... "

The PAM brought Mad Magnet. He zapped passersby with his magnetic beams, and stuck them to each other like some sort of weird living sculpture.

Shane was in the Storm Chargers store when he heard the panic outside. Mad Magnet shot a powerful ray at Shane, which magnetized him and pulled him through a wall into an empty warehouse.

Back at Ninja Ops, Cam watched on his view screen.

"Shane's up against some weird thing with a magnet for a head," he told Tori and Dustin.

"We'd better help him," said Tori.

But Sensei held up his paw. "Wait. I will tell you when it is time. Shane must learn to ask for help."

Back in the warehouse, Shane called on the only help he could.

"Ninja Storm, Ranger Form!" he yelled, morphing into Red Ranger. "Power of Air. Get ready to be recycled, tin head."

"But where are your friends, Ranger?" asked Mad Magnet.

"I don't need them," said Red – but he thought better of that statement when Mad Magnet fired a pulse from his head that surrounded him in green electricity. It drew him towards an old car and crashed him into it.

"I can't handle this thing alone," said Red Ranger. "Tori, Dustin, I REALLY need your help."

Dustin looked from the view screen to Sensei. "Now?" he asked.

Sensei nodded. "Now."

"Ninja Storm, Ranger Form!" cried Tori and Dustin, and in a micro-second they morphed into Blue and Yellow Rangers.

"Power of Water," said Blue Ranger.

"Power of Earth," said Yellow.

Then they were gone.

When Yellow and Blue Rangers arrived at the warehouse, their attack on Mad Magnet was short, but ended with him flying through a wall.

"You guys came," said Red Ranger. "Even after I said all those stupid things."

"Of course we came," said Blue Ranger.

"I was a jerk," said Red. "I need you guys. We're a team, right?"

"Right."

Just then, Mad Magnet attacked again.

"New plan," said Red Ranger. "Ninja air assault!"

He ran at the monster, leapt up, and kicked him out of the warehouse again.

KA-BOOM!!

KICK!!

HA-ZAP!! **HA-ZAP!!**

AAAGGGHHH!!

All three Rangers followed up the attack with their swords. But Mad Magnet pulled out a lightning sword and blasted back at them.

Red Ranger pointed to an energy pulse in the monster's chest. "Let's take out his energy centre."

As Mad Magnet moved in once again, the Rangers called up their special weapons.

"Lion Hammer!" said Yellow Ranger.

"Sonic Fin!" said Blue Ranger.

"Hawk Blaster!" said Red Ranger.

"Put them together, and what do you get?" asked Blue Ranger.

ZZZZ!! **SSST!!**

"STORM STRIKER!" they yelled, and the weapons joined together to make one.

This time there could be no doubt about Mad Magnet's fate ... or could there?

Watching events from his space lair, Lothor decided to send help ...

The Scroll of Empowerment sped from the spaceship to Earth, and suddenly Mad Magnet grew to giant size. He towered over the Rangers, and lifted a huge foot as if to crush them.

This was serious. "Send the Zords," Sensei told Cam.

Cam spoke to the Rangers. "Guys, I'm sending you some big-time backup," he told them. "Hawk Zord, Dolphin Zord and Lion Zord. Command them using your inner Ninja powers of Air, Water and Earth. They have state of the art weapons."

ZZZZ!!

BZZZ-ZZAM!!

As he spoke, the Rangers saw the mighty Zords approaching.

"Shane, you pilot Hawk Zord," said Cam. "Tori, use your power of water to command Dolphin Zord, and Dustin, Lion Zord is yours."

Yellow Ranger spoke for all of them. "Wow! Massive, dude!"

The Rangers were seriously impressed, but Mad Magnet remained defiant. "You think you can stop me with things made of metal?" he asked. "I'm a magnet, remember!"

He blasted powerful green laser beams from his head that rocked the Zords.

"Flame attack," said Red Ranger, and Hawk Zord turned into a flying flame that licked around the monster's head.

Dolphin Zord smashed into Mad Magnet and tossed him into the air, then smacked him away with her tail.

WOOOSSHH!!

SPLASSHH!!

But Mad Magnet still wasn't beaten. His two massive magnet hands reached up, and grabbed Hawk Zord and Dolphin Zord.

Now it was Yellow Ranger's turn. "Lion Tornado Blast!" he cried, and Lion Zord changed into a powerful fan that blew Red and Blue free. "Now let's show him some real muscle. Afterburners – fire!"

Yellow Ranger made a wind tunnel and sailed through it, crashing into Mad Magnet with such force that he was blown into a million tiny pieces. "Magnet dude, you are headed for the scrap heap!"

But as the Rangers watched, the monster re-formed!

"I don't know what we do now," said Red Ranger.

Sensei appeared on his screen. "Feel what is inside you," he said.

Suddenly, Red Ranger remembered something that told him what to do. "The scroll!" he said. "One has the strength of three ..."

He pressed switches, and the three Zords came together as one giant Megazord which came under immediate attack from Mad Magnet's laser beams.

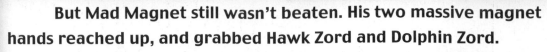

WWWHIRR!!

RRRUMBLE!!

SSST!!

BOOM!BOOM!!

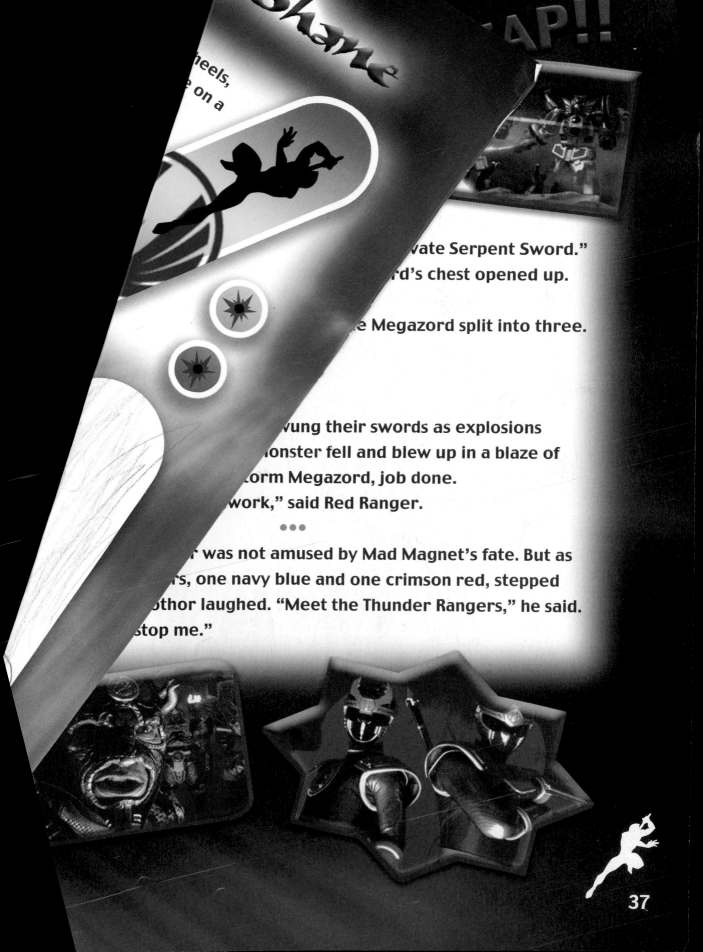

vate Serpent Sword."

rd's chest opened up.

e Megazord split into three.

...vung their swords as explosions

...onster fell and blew up in a blaze of

...torm Megazord, job done.

...work," said Red Ranger.

● ● ●

...r was not amused by Mad Magnet's fate. But as

...rs, one navy blue and one crimson red, stepped

...othor laughed. "Meet the Thunder Rangers," he said.

...stop me."

Shane loves being on four w
just as long as the wheels ar
skateboard.

He's always on the lookout for cool new boards
and wheels, so why not use these blanks to try
out some new designs for him? Maybe you
could design one to match his Red Wind
Ranger outfit, or base some on his sky
and stars powers?

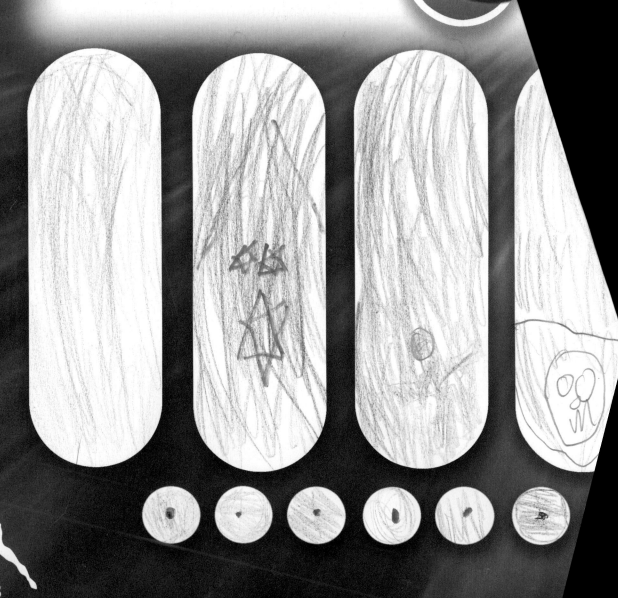

ZZZZ!!

AAAHH!!

HA-ZAP!!

"Move to a new power level," said Cam. "Activate Serpent Sword."

The Rangers did as he said, and the Megazord's chest opened up. A large ball shot out and turned into a sword.

"Megazord, multiply!" said Cam, and the Megazord split into three.

"Ready," said Red Ranger.

"Aim," said Blue Ranger.

"FIRE!" said Yellow Ranger.

The three Storm Megazords swung their swords as explosions shook Mad Magnet. Then, as the monster fell and blew up in a blaze of flames, they phased back into Storm Megazord, job done.

"That's what I call teamwork," said Red Ranger.

• • •

Out in space, Lothor was not amused by Mad Magnet's fate. But as two shiny metal Rangers, one navy blue and one crimson red, stepped from the shadows, Lothor laughed. "Meet the Thunder Rangers," he said. "Now, no one will stop me."

Boarding with Shane

Shane loves being on four wheels, just as long as the wheels are on a skateboard.

He's always on the lookout for cool new boards and wheels, so why not use these blanks to try out some new designs for him? Maybe you could design one to match his Red Wind Ranger outfit, or base some on his sky and stars powers?

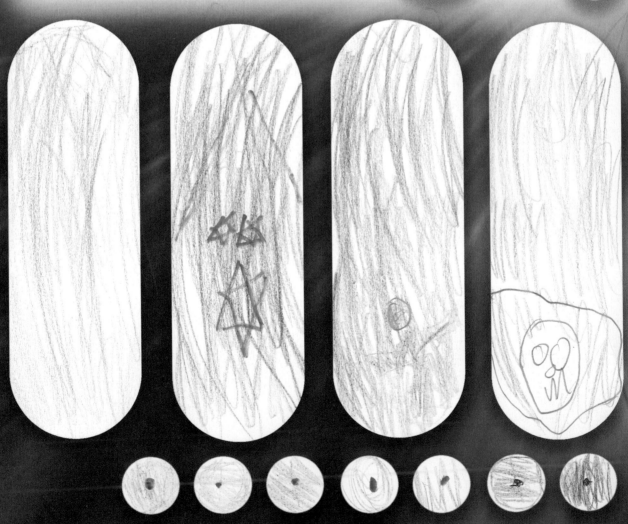

Shane's just loving the new skate park, and he can't wait to try out the big ramp. But which is the only route that leads to the ramp?

Know Your Enemy

Lothor has just one plan and one aim: to take total control of the planet Earth, and all its inhabitants.

Once called Kiya, he was a student at the Wind Ninja Academy. When he used dark Ninja magic, his twin brother Kanoi tried to stop him. Kiya was expelled from the Academy and was sent out into deep space. But before he went, he swore to take his revenge, and took a new name, Lothor.

Lurking on–board his mighty spaceship, Lothor learned even more dark powers, and now he plans to use them against his enemies, the Ninjas.

The first part of Lothor's plan – to destroy the Wind Ninja Academy – was successful, but his attack did not kill his brother, who is now Sensei. He and his pupils, the Wind Rangers, are the only ones left who may be able to stop Lothor.

Zurgane and **Choobo** form part of Lothor's evil force. Zurgane takes his job of taking over the Earth very seriously, and will do anything to make sure it happens. Choobo tries to be like him, but can't be serious for too long.

Lothor's huge army is made up of soldiers called **Kelzaks**. They are skilled in the use of fighting clubs and swords. They appear in a flash, as if out of nowhere – and disappear just as fast. No matter how many of them are defeated, there are always more to fight on.

Kapri is one of Lothor's nieces. She's mean and bossy, and is always telling her sister **Marah** what to do. Both girls help their uncle by summoning up monsters – and making them grow into giants.

Thunder Strangers

One day, Cam asked the Rangers to check out some strange heat readings at the quarry. There, they were attacked by two strangers. "Old Rangers out, new Rangers in," said one of them.

They were Crimson Thunder Ranger and Navy Thunder Ranger and they and their Zords, Crimson Insectazord and Navy Beetlezord, were working with Lothor!

When Amphibidor, a frog monster, attacked Tori, a new friend of hers called Blake Bradley arrived to help her. But he ended up injured so Tori took him to Ninja Ops. What she didn't know – but was about to find out! – was that Blake was really Navy Thunder Ranger!

Later, when Crimson Thunder Ranger and Navy Thunder Ranger appeared again, the Rangers were amazed to see them de-morph into Blake and his brother, Hunter! The two of them disappeared again – but they took Sensei with them, trapped in his energy ball! The Rangers followed them to the Mountain of Lost Ninjas, to the Cavern of Spirits.

They begged Blake and Hunter not to destroy Sensei, but the brothers said he must die because he had killed their parents years before – and they wanted revenge!

At that moment the ghosts of their parents appeared, and told their sons that it was Lothor who had killed them, not Sensei!

Now the Thunder Rangers knew the truth they vowed to join the Wind Rangers in the fight against their old ally, Lothor. The Thunder and Ninja Zords would join together, too, as the Thunderstorm Megazord.

"Sky of Wonder!"
"Power of Thunder!"

Now three Rangers were five ...

POWER RANGERS PROFILE

FULL NAME:

Hunter Bradley

RANGER DESIGNATION:

Crimson Thunder Ranger

ZORD:	Insectizord
WEAPONS:	Crimson Blaster, Thunder Staff
GEAR:	Thunder Morpher, Tsunami Cycle
SPORTS:	Motocross

CHARACTER:

Hunter can seem rather intense, but that's because he has a strong sense of honour. When he first joined forces with the Wind Rangers he challenged Shane as leader, but now he's learned that there are times to lead – and times to follow.

SKILLS:

Hunter loves motocross and his job helping out at the Storm Chargers extreme sports store. Like his riding, his fighting style is fast and fearless. He uses the power of thunder and pilots the Crimson Insectizord.

"Power of Thunder!"

When an enemy strikes, Crimson Thunder Ranger can call upon Insectizord to help him.

Use the small picture of Insectizord to help you colour the larger one.

POWER RANGERS PROFILE

FULL NAME:

Blake Bradley

RANGER DESIGNATION:

Navy Thunder Ranger

ZORD: Beetlezord

WEAPONS: Navy Antler, Thunder Staff

GEAR: Thunder Morpher, Tsunami Cycle

SPORTS: Motocross

CHARACTER:

Blake has a real sense of what's right and what's wrong. When he was fighting with Lothor against the Wind Rangers, he used Tori to get into Ninja Ops – but he didn't feel too good about acting that way, because he likes Tori a lot.

SKILLS:

Like his brother Hunter, Blake loves speed, and they both count motocross racing as their favourite sport. Blake is a skilled Ninja fighter, and uses the special power of thunder. He's the pilot of the Navy Beetlezord.

"Power of Thunder!"

When an enemy strikes, Navy Thunder Ranger can call upon Beetlezord to help him.

Use the small picture of Beetlezord to help you colour the larger one.

The Samurai's Journey

Far out in space, Zurgane had a new monster for his master, Lothor.

"Meet Madtropolis," said Zurgane. "He has the power to create the illusion that he is another being."

"Nice party trick," said Lothor.

"But there's more," Zurgane replied, as the monster held out a strange ball-shaped container.

"With this, I can capture the Rangers' energy," said Madtropolis. "The Earth will be defenceless."

"Ah, I see ..." said Lothor.

•••

At Ninja class, Sensei chopped a marble block in half with his paw.

His pupils tried – and failed – to copy him, and were rubbing sore hands when they heard a cry, and turned to see Cam split the marble.

"That's gotta be a trick," said Hunter.

"Just because I'm not a Ranger doesn't mean I'm useless!" said Cam, and he stalked out, followed by Tori.

"You all right?" she asked.

"Yeah, just tired of the lack of respect," said Cam.

"But Cam, everything we do is because of what you do."

"It's not enough," said Cam. "I want to be a Ranger, but Dad won't allow it."

"Tell him how you feel," said Tori. "Go talk to him."

Cam smiled. "OK. But if he doesn't listen, I'm not cleaning out his cage again!"

Suddenly, Madtropolis, Kapri, Marah and a troop of Kelzaks appeared.

"Attack!" yelled Kapri, and Madtropolis let loose a powerful blast that brought the other Rangers running.

"Ninja Storm!" cried Shane, Tori and Dustin.

"Thunder Storm!" cried Blake and Hunter.

Then they spoke as one: "Ranger Form!" and morphed into Rangers.

"Power of Earth," said Yellow Ranger.

"Air," said Red.

"Water," said Blue.

"Power of Thunder," said Navy Ranger.

Crimson Ranger was about to speak when Madtropolis attacked again. "Cam, run!"

"No way!" said Cam, running at the Kelzaks. "I can help!"

But Cam was no match for so many Kelzaks, and could only watch as Madtropolis opened the container – and sucked the Rangers' colours into it!

As their suits faded to grey, they de-morphed, and slid to the ground.

The sphere pulsed with the Rangers' stolen energy. "See you, Power Losers!" said Madtropolis – and vanished into thin air!

•••

Later, back at Ninja Ops, Cam told the Rangers what had happened. "He drained your Ranger energy."

"Then we need to get it back," said Shane. "Come on."

"OK," said Cam, hitting the computer. "I'll give you a power boost – but it won't last."

•••

The Rangers found Madtropolis in an empty warehouse. "Now to destroy the Rangers' powers," he said, and laughed – until Red Ranger snatched the container from him.

Red Ranger fired his Hawk Blaster, but Madtropolis used his powers to vanish – and reappear behind Shane.

Then suddenly, Red Ranger found himself in a dark dimension.

"Ninja sword!" he yelled.

Red Ranger slashed at the monster, or what looked like the monster. But he actually hit Navy and Crimson Rangers!

"I thought I was fighting Madtropolis," said Red Ranger.

"So did we," said Navy.

Seconds later, the Rangers were fighting each other again. Then Blue and Yellow gaped as THREE Madtropolises appeared, and transformed into Red, Crimson and Navy Rangers.

"Can't tell what's real and what's not?" sneered Madtropolis, before vanishing again ...

Sensei was watching events back at Ninja Ops. "Trust your heart, Red Ranger," he said. "Your inner Ninja will tell you what is real and what is not."

"I'll try," said Shane. He concentrated hard, and shot Madtropolis. This time it was the real thing, but he was soon back again.

"Thunder Storm cannon!" cried the Rangers, forming Storm Striker. But before they could fire, the single monster became an army of monsters.

"FIRE!" yelled Red Ranger, and the clones disappeared, and the real monster sizzled ...

But he wasn't finished. Lothor sent the Scroll of Empowerment to Earth and, as it unrolled, Madtropolis transformed again, this time into an enormous giant.

The Rangers tried to open the container to release their energy, but failed.

Back at base, Cam pushed a button, and the container was teleported to Ninja Ops. Then he sent the Thunder and Storm Megazords to help. "I'm sending some protection," he said, and a Power Sphere in the form of a red cloth appeared.

"You sent us a scarf?" said Red Ranger.

Cam paused. "Just go with it."

But even with the protection, the Rangers had no strength left. Tossed out of the Megazord, they hit the ground, de-morphed and lay motionless.

"Say goodbye, Rangers!" said Madtropolis.

Cam watched, helpless. "What can we do?" he asked.

"There was a power mighty enough to help us," said Sensei. "But that was in the past. Now, we cannot predict how the portal will ..."

"The Scroll of Time!" said Cam.

"No, you must not!" said Sensei.

"But I have to," said Cam. "I have to go back in time, back to the past, to get the one power source that can help us."

Sensei knew he was right. He bowed to his son, and stepped aside as Cam took the Scroll of Time ...

As he did so, the Earth shuddered and shook, and the Rangers and Madtropolis froze.

"Our time will be frozen until the writing on the scroll fades," said Sensei. "You must hurry, or you will be trapped in the past." He paused. "For ever."

Cam unrolled the scroll and a strange portal opened. He looked at his father, and stepped through ...

Cam was hurled through a tunnel of light and sound. When he opened his eyes, he was at the waterfall near the Academy.

"It looks the same," he said, looking around. "Did it work?"

Suddenly, a Wind Academy Ninja appeared.

Cam was about to find out.

(continued on page 54)

Surfing with Tori

Tori loves surfing, and spends all her spare time out on the ocean, riding the biggest waves she can find.

Can you help her navigate through the big breakers to the shore?

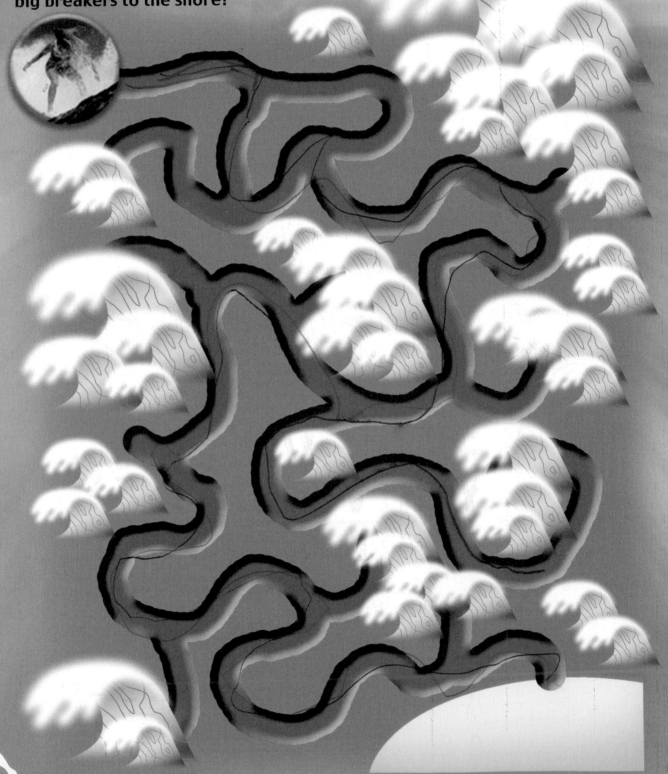

Can you find all these words in Tori's surfing word search? They are spelled out from left to right, and from top to bottom.

SURF	BOARD
WATER	BREAKER
OCEAN	WAVE
SEA	SPORT
TIDE	SPRAY

S	E	B	O	A	R	D	Z
P	F	R	C	D	K	X	S
O	C	E	A	N	L	H	P
R	J	A	S	U	R	F	R
T	B	K	W	M	I	P	A
A	S	E	A	Q	R	O	Y
G	Y	R	V	T	I	D	E
W	A	T	E	R	N	O	S

Well done!

53

The Samurai's Journey

The Ninja took Cam to an old Sensei master. "Take him to join the new students, Kanoi," the master told him.

"Kanoi?" said Cam. He stared hard. "You remind me of someone."

"Follow me," said Kanoi.

Cam knew who the Ninja was. He was his father when he was a young man.

"I'm coming ... Father," whispered Cam.

●●●

Sensei transported the Rangers back to Ninja Ops. They were weak, but safe.

He explained where Cam had gone. "He has gone back in time to get help. If he is not back before time resumes, I fear we will be unable to prevent Madtropolis destroying our planet. Cam is on a journey that may decide the fate of the whole world."

●●●

In the past, Cam watched as Kanoi demonstrated his impressive sword skills.

"He can be beaten," another student whispered. "I should know. I'm Kiya, Kanoi's twin."

Cam stared. He looked like another young version of his father!

The next part of the demonstration involved Kanoi fighting with another new student, who was fast and agile, with the rare skills of a Samurai.

The new student defeated Kanoi easily.

"Excellent, Miko," said Sensei, as the new student pulled off her mask.

Cam stared. He recognised the girl. It was his mother ...

"A girl!" said Kanoi. "Her sword work is not the Wind Ninja way!"

"I was trained as a Samurai by my father," said Miko.

"But no women are allowed here!" said Kanoi, still smarting from his defeat.

"Why?" asked Kiya. "Maybe that needs to change."

The old Sensei stepped forward. "Enough!" he said. "Miko will be the first female student in the school's history."

"Thank you, Sensei," said Miko, as Kanoi stalked off in disgust.

Later, Kiya was watching as Miko trained and a pendant with a green jade amulet slipped from her robe.

Kiya's eyes went to it. "May I look?" he asked.

Miko pulled away. "No, sorry. It's a family piece. I ..."

Kiya held Miko's gaze. His eyes turned black as he stared hard, using dark Ninja powers.

"Let ... me ... see ... it," he said, reaching for the charm, which crackled with energy.

At that moment, Cam stepped out of the bushes. "Am I interrupting something?" he asked.

His words broke Kiya's concentration – and his dark spell. He turned away. "We'll talk later."

"How did you learn those sword moves?" asked Cam.

Miko touched the green charm. "The Samurai spirit has been passed down through my family with the amulet," she told him. "It was given to me by my father."

When Miko went into her tent, Cam took the Scroll of Time from his robe. The letters on it, which had started to fade, now glowed with new energy. "I get it," said Cam to himself. "The letters are stronger when I'm near Miko's amulet. But what am I supposed to do about it?"

• • •

Later, Cam was still wondering about the amulet's powers when Miko flew at him and pinned him to the ground!

"Where is it?" she cried.

"Where's what?" asked Cam.

"My amulet, of course!" said Miko. "I saw someone take it from my tent. It was you! I recognise the uniform."

55

Kanoi arrived with some of the students. "I'm captain of the Academy Guard," he said, grabbing Cam's arm. "You're under arrest."

"What?" said Cam.

As the guards marched off with Cam, Kanoi saw a green glow in the undergrowth and went to take a look ...

Back at the Academy, the old Sensei confronted Cam. "You are accused of stealing," he said. "The law is clear. Anyone guilty of breaking the Ninja code must be banished. My verdict is that you are ..."

"Not guilty!" said Kanoi, stepping forward with the amulet in one hand, and a student wearing the same uniform as Cam in the other. It was Kiya!

"I caught him in the woods," said Kanoi. "He was trying to use dark Ninja powers to unlock the amulet."

Kiya looked hard at Kanoi, then used a blast of dark energy to knock him to the ground. He aimed another blast at Miko – but not before she had tossed the amulet to Cam.

Kiya raised his hand, and set up a force field around Cam and himself.

They fought furiously. Kiya was winning when the green charm around Cam's neck came to life. As it glowed, Kiya was blasted high into the air, breaking the force field.

Cam touched the amulet and a green energy beam streaked towards Kiya. He slumped to the ground.

Cam looked at the amulet. "What happened?"

"The Samurai amulet has found its owner," said Miko. "It's what you came here for, isn't it?"

Before Cam could reply, Kiya spoke. "You will not stop me using dark powers!" he cried. "I will rule this world."

"No, you will be expelled, cast out into space, where your dark powers can do no harm," said Sensei. "Kiya no longer exists."

As he spoke a magical sphere appeared, trapping Kiya inside.

"I no longer need that name," said Kiya. "From now on I take the name of the ancient warrior of evil – LOTHOR!"

"Begone," said Sensei, and the magic ball shrank, then blasted off into deep space.

As Cam watched, the Scroll of Time fell to the ground, and the time portal opened.

"It is time for you to go," said Sensei.

"Use the amulet," said Miko.

Then the portal closed, and Cam was on his way through time again ...

●●●

At Ninja Ops, the Rangers started to fade. "You will return to where you were when time stopped," Sensei explained, and in a split second they found themselves under attack by Madtropolis again.

He was just about to crush them, when the Emerald Wind Helicopter appeared.

Green Ranger Samurai fired a hail of lasers and rockets that cut open the ground around Madtropolis and he dropped down into the Earth.

"Star Samurai Megazord!" said Green Ranger, and the helicopter transformed, hovering over Madtropolis.

"Bee spinner – locked and dropped," said Green Ranger.

A Power Sphere appeared in the Megazord's hands and a bee–like weapon streaked out. It hit Madtropolis, and he exploded into a million fragments.

The Megazord landed and, when the smoke cleared, Dustin spoke. "Is it me, or is that a guy in Green Ranger gear?"

"That's right, Dustin," said Green Ranger.

"Hey, how do you know my name?" asked Dustin.

The Green Ranger de–morphed and smiled.

It was Cam!

(continued on page 60)

Racing with Dustin

Dustin's a real speed freak! He's a big fan of fast extreme sports – and as far as he's concerned, you can't get faster or more extreme than motocross. Thunder Rangers Blake and Hunter are keen on motocross too, so the three of them often race against each other.

Find out which Ranger will win the race by playing this game with friends.

You need a dice and a counter each.
Choose to play as Blake, Hunter or Dustin, and put your rider's counter on the start.
Take turns to roll the dice, and move along the track. If you roll 2, move 2 spaces, and so on.
If you land on a track section with a red flag, miss a turn.
If you land on a track section with a green flag, have an extra turn.
The first rider to reach the finish wins the race.

START

1
2
3
4
5
6
7
8
9
10
11
12

The Samurai's Journey

The Rangers' energy was almost gone. "We have to get you back to Ninja Ops," Cam told them. But before they could move, Lothor attacked. He hovered in the air, firing hard, then Marah, Kapri and an army of Kelzaks joined him.

"Hello, Nephew," Lothor said to Cam.

"Did he say nephew?" asked Dustin.

Cam shook his head. "Don't ask."

Lothor and his troops closed in, but suddenly the Rangers all disappeared into thin air, leaving Lothor screaming in anger. Sensei had teleported them back to Ninja Ops just in time.

"If we'd had our powers, we could have taken him," said Shane.

"Then it is time you got your powers back," said Sensei. "But the sphere holds the power of five Rangers, and only an even greater power can open it."

"Like the greater power of six Rangers?" said Dustin, looking at Cam, who held out his hand over the sphere. The other Rangers added their hands to the stack, and energy grew inside. Then the jar opened!

The Rangers had their powers back – and there was a new Ranger, too!

Tori spoke the question they all wanted to ask: "How did all this happen?"

It was time for Cam to tell them about his travels through time ...

● ● ●

Out in his space lair, Lothor was planning his next attack. He was planning to unleash a new collection of five mighty aliens against Earth – and the Rangers.

"Zurgane," he growled. "Let Operation Alien Outreach begin. This time, there will be no escape."

● ● ●

Seconds later, at Ninja Ops, alarms blared and monitors came to life. There were reports of aliens all over the city!

"Rangers, GO!" said Sensei.

Red and Yellow Rangers flew into the city on hang-gliders to fight aliens called Sky Scrapper and Hip-Hopper.

Navy Ranger went to the beach on Thunder Cycle to tackle Tentacreep.

Blue Ranger fought against a monster called Starvark, and Crimson had an alien magician called Magic Moustache to deal with.

Lothor was pleased with what he saw on the monitors. "Excellent," he said. "With the others kept busy, Green Ranger will be forced to face my most dangerous alien of all."

Up stepped a giant mosquito. "The name's Sucker," it said. "At your service."

"And what alien powers do you have?" asked Zurgane.

"I can turn any living being into a bug with a little prick of my proboscis," said Sucker. "That's my nose."

"Perfect," said Lothor.

●●●

Back at Ninja Ops, Sensei and Cam watched as Sucker stalked the city.

"Dad?" said Cam.

Sensei nodded. "Go."

Cam smiled. "Samurai Storm, Ranger Form," he chanted as he morphed. "Green Samurai Power!"

Moments later Green Samurai Ranger heard a buzzing noise, and Sucker buzzed around him, biting at him.

"You will feel my sting!" said Sucker as, right on cue, Kelzaks appeared out of nowhere. They held Green Ranger down as Sucker grew to human size, moved towards him – and bit hard!

"That hurt!" said Green Ranger. He fought back, kicking at Sucker, then using his sword skills to scatter the Kelzaks.

●●●

In other parts of the city, the Rangers were fighting their own battles. But as soon as they blew up the monsters, they reappeared!

"Return to Ninja Ops," said Sensei. "We must regroup."

●●●

Out in space, Lothor realised that this was his big chance. "I must strike now!" he told Zurgane. "Make the monsters grow. I need big ones!"

"But you can only make one monster at a time grow," said Zurgane.

"What?" said Lothor. "Then make one grow – Starvark."

●●●

At Ninja Ops, all eyes were on the monitor as Starvark grew to a gigantic size.

"We'll get the Zords," said Shane.

Seconds later the Megazord went into battle against Starvark, swinging the Ram Hammer Turtle Mace at the giant alien.

Lothor's alien needed help. "Scroll of Empowerment – descend!" ordered Zurgane, and down on Earth the scroll unrolled into Magic Moustache.

●●●

Back at Ninja Ops, strange things were happening to Cam. Coarse hairs were starting to grow all over his body, and he was changing colour. Sensei checked him out.

"Sucker's bite injected a deadly toxin into your body," he told his son. "It is turning you into an insect."

"My first battle and I get changed into a bug!" said Cam. "What do we do?"

"Only the alien can remove the toxin," said Sensei. "You must make Sucker take it back."

When Green Ranger found Sucker, he yelled, "Samurai Ranger full power! Super Samurai mode!"

Green Ranger took Sucker's beak and slammed it onto his own chest. When the alien insect breathed in, it took all the toxin back from Green Ranger.

As the toxin drained out of him, Green Ranger looked up into space. He knew that Lothor would be watching from his lair. "Like that, Uncle?" he asked.

Lothor fumed, and ordered Zurgane to make Sucker grow this time.

"Scroll of Empowerment – descend," ordered Zurgane.

On Earth the scroll unrolled as Sucker grew and grew.

"Oh–oh," said Green Ranger as Sucker moved in to attack the Megazord, which used the Ram Hammer against the giant insect. But now Sucker was more powerful than ever, and when it ran at the Megazord, the Zord crashed to the ground.

"Say goodbye, Rangers," said Sucker. It raised its arm to strike – but fell to the ground in a hail of sparks.

Green Ranger had attacked with the Samurai Star Megazord!

"Samurai Storm Formation!" he cried, and his Megazord attached to the Storm Megazord. Its arm shot out a power beam that cut right through Sucker, and the alien shattered.

Green Ranger looked around, and smiled. "Not bad for my first day on the job!"

● ● ●

When Cam walked into Ninja Ops later, the other Rangers were there.

"What are you all smiling about?" he asked.

Shane held up a brand new Samurai Ninja Ops uniform. "If you're gonna be part of the team, you gotta have the right gear," he said. "Here."

Cam took the uniform and held it against himself. A big grin spread across his face. "Thanks, guys."

Sensei had the last word, as usual. "No father could be prouder of his son."

The End

POWER RANGERS PROFILE

FULL NAME:

Cameron Watanabe

RANGER DESIGNATION:

Green Samurai Ranger

ZORD: Samurai Star

WEAPONS: Samurai Sabre

GEAR: Samurai Cyclone Morpher

INTERESTS: Computers

CHARACTER:

Cameron (Cam to his friends) is the real brains behind the Rangers team. He can be rather sarcastic, and he doesn't always have a great sense of humour. But he's a great model of discipline and focus.

SKILLS:

Cam has the most highly developed martial arts skills of all the Rangers. His Samurai Sabre is linked to the Ninja Ops computers, so he can control the Zords and monitor events. He can also boost his power up into Super Samurai Mode.

"Power of the Samurai!"

Use the small picture of Green Samurai Ranger
to help you colour the larger one.

Sensei's Skills Tests

Even though he is now in the form of a guinea pig, Sensei is still wise and all-knowing. He has tried to teach the Power Rangers the skills they will need if they are to defend the Earth and all its people against Lothor and his army.

Sensei knows that the Rangers need the very special fighting skills of the Ninja. But he knows how important other skills are, too.

Test your own abilities with Sensei's skills tests, and see if you've got what it takes to be a Power Ranger. The answers are on page 69.

1. COMMUNICATION TEST

Can you decipher Sensei's coded message for the Rangers? Write a letter for each number.

1	2	3	4	5	6	7	8	9	10	11	12	13	14	15	16	17	18	19	20	21	22	23	24	25	26
p	z	t	k	l	a	j	n	g	h	q	e	c	b	m	x	y	f	i	v	o	w	d	u	s	r

25	3	26	21	8	9	12	26		6	25		21	8	12
s	t	r	o	n	g	e	r		a	s		o	n	e

3	10	6	8		3	10	26	12	12
t	h	a	n		T	h	r	e	e

SCORE 1 POINT FOR EACH CORRECT WORD.

66

2. OBSERVATION TEST

These pictures of Green Samurai Ranger are all the same – or are they? In fact, all of them are holograms except one. Look very carefully. Can you identify the real Green Ranger?

1

2

3

4

5

6

SCORE 5 POINTS FOR A CORRECT ANSWER.

Well done! Are you ready for your next test?

Can you write a number and a letter to link each Ranger and their Zord?

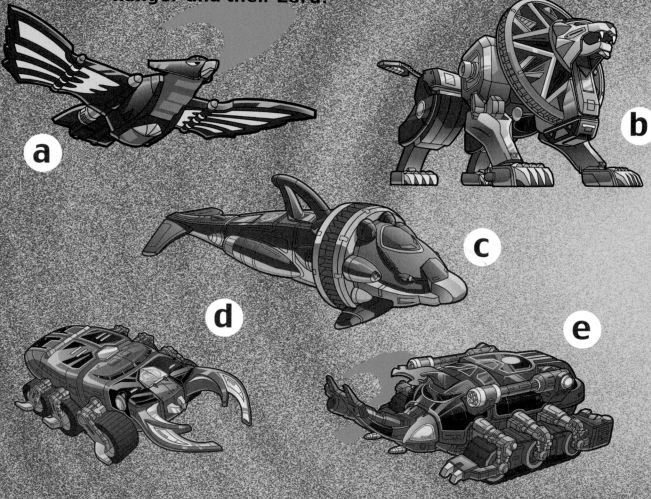

a

b

c

d

e

Red Power Ranger	a	5		**1** BEETLEZORD
Blue Power Ranger	c	4		**2** INSECTIZORD
Yellow Power Ranger	b	3		**3** LION ZORD
Crimson Power Ranger		2		**4** DOLPHIN ZORD
Navy Power Ranger		1		**5** HAWK ZORD

SCORE 1 POINT FOR EACH CORRECT ANSWER.

There is one final test before you complete your training. Answer these five questions; all the answers can be found in this annual, but see if you can remember them without looking!
1. What sport does Tori like?
2. What is Dustin's real first name?
3. What are Lothor's soldiers called?
4. Which Ranger is Blake Bradley?
5. Who is Cam's father?
SCORE 1 POINT FOR EACH CORRECT ANSWER.

Answers:
1 . C O M M U N I C A T I O N   T E S T
stronger as one than three
2 . O B S E R V A T I O N   T E S T
4; the sword is longer
3 . I D E N T I F I C A T I O N   T E S T

Red Power Ranger	a	5
Blue Power Ranger	c	4
Yellow Power Ranger	b	3
Crimson Power Ranger	e	2
Navy Power Ranger	d	1

4 . K N O W L E D G E   T E S T
1. Surfing 2. Waldo 3. Kelzaks 4. Navy Thunder Ranger 5. Sensei

Write your scores here and add up the total:

C O M M U N I C A T I O N T E S T	yes
O B S E R V A T I O N T E S T	yes
I D E N T I F I C A T I O N T E S T	yes
K N O W L E D G E T E S T	yes
T O T A L	20 OUT OF 20

You scored the 20 maximum? Hey, what a result! Award yourself special Power Ranger status – you've earned it. Fill in your name, decide on your personal Ranger, weapon and equipment names, and add a picture or drawing of the newest Power Ranger.

Name: _Sam_
Ranger name: _Red samri_
Weapon: _Sod Fire Sord_
Gear: _Red Starng_
Zord: _Red samri Stor_

Welcome to the Academy!